LITTLE MONSTER

Story by
BARRIE WADE
Pictures by
KATINKA KEW

Lothrop, Lee & Shepard Books
New York

For Ed and Pat

Text copyright © 1990 by Barrie Wade
Illustrations copyright © 1990 by Katinka Kew
First published in Great Britain by Andre Deutsch, Ltd.
All rights reserved. No part of this book may be reproduced or utilized in any form or by any means,
electronic or mechanical, including photocopying, recording or by any information storage and
retrieval system, without permission in writing from the Publisher. Inquiries should be addressed to
Lothrop, Lee & Shepard Books, a division of William Morrow & Company, Inc., 105 Madison Avenue,
New York, New York 10016
Printed in Belgium
First U.S. edition 1 2 3 4 5 6 7 8 9 10

Library of Congress Cataloging in Publication Data
Wade, Barrie. Little monster / story by Barrie Wade; pictures by Katinka Kew.   p.   cm.
Summary: Mandy, who is usually perfectly behaved, tries acting naughty and finds that her mother
still loves her. ISBN 0-688-09596-8.—ISBN 0-688-09597-6 (lib. bdg.) [1. Behavior—Fiction.]
I. Kew, Katinka, ill. II. Title. PZ7.W1139L1 1990 [E]—dc20 89-37277 CIP AC

Mandy was awake when her parents'
friends came over. She crept downstairs.

She heard her mother telling her friends,
"My Mandy is as good as gold. My Mandy
is never noisy, never untidy, never dirty,
never rude, and never disobedient."

"My Mandy is perfect," said her mother,

and Mandy smiled.

"But my Jimmy is a little monster,"
Mandy's mother went on. "He's just like
his father." Mandy's mother laughed, and
so did everybody else.

All except Mandy.

She crept back upstairs.

Just then there was a dreadful crash in Jimmy's room.

Mandy's mother came running. From the sound of her voice, Mandy knew she was cross.

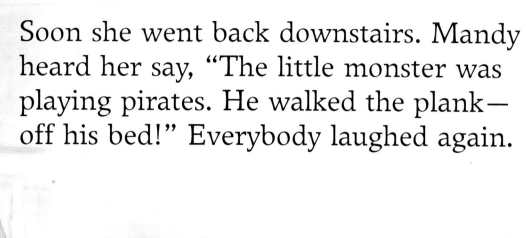

Soon she went back downstairs. Mandy heard her say, "The little monster was playing pirates. He walked the plank—off his bed!" Everybody laughed again.

Mandy folded her clothes.

She washed her face.

She brushed her teeth.

She combed her hair.

She tucked herself in.

Next morning Mandy did not make
her bed

or fold her pajamas.

She trampled her father's garden

and tracked mud into the kitchen.

After lunch she roared like a lion at Jimmy

and made him cry.

At dinner she stuck her tongue out

and made a rude noise.

When her mother called her at bedtime,

she was hiding in the garden.

"Come in at once," said her mother. Her voice sounded angry.

"I won't!" cried Mandy, and she stamped her foot.

"You little monster," cried her mother.
Mandy smiled.

Her mother smiled back. Then she
started to laugh.

"I love you, little Mandy," she said.

"Even when I'm naughty?" asked Mandy.
"Even when you're naughty," her mother replied.

Mandy's mother tucked her into bed, and
Mandy was as good as gold.